THE MIMES OF THE
COURTESANS LUCIAN

TRANSLATOR'S FOREWORD

In view of the constantly changing standards for adequate translations, the task of the translator is not an easy one. A rendition which a few years ago might have been entirely satisfactory would now be considered literal, stilted and uninspired. And so, in our modern requirements for an effective version, something more is demanded than a merely accurate translation of words or even phrases; instead, a genuine appreciation of atmosphere, spirit and intent is insisted upon.

The Mimes of the Courtesans presents no exception to this perpetual problem of the translator. In fact, the task is intensified in this case because of the informality of the dialogues and the racy, whimsical style in which they are written. The frequent occurrence of colloquialisms, of intimate and subtle humor, requires an ease and freedom in translation not permissible, perhaps, in works of scholarly import.

The translator has endeavored to keep constantly in mind the kindly humanism with which Lucian wrote these tales so descriptive of one phase of Greek life. Lucian discusses intimate sex details with the frankness of one not immoral, but influenced by a system of morals that finds everything that is natural both beautiful and good.

These dialogues can hardly be offensive to the intelligent modern; for, somehow, our own civilization is changing, and as it becomes richer and fuller, it seems to have more in common with the civilizations of antiquity.

A. L. H.

October 1, 1928.

CONTENTS

THE EDUCATION OF CORINNA

CORINNA, a little girl
CROBYLE, her mother

THE EDUCATION OF CORINNA

CROBYLE

Well, Corinna, you see now that it wasn't so terrible to lose your virginity. You have spent your first night with a man. You have earned your first gift, no less than a hundred drachmas. With that I'll buy you a necklace.

CORINNA

Yes, dear mother, do buy me a necklace. Let it be a necklace made of fine, shining stones like the one Philainis wears.

CROBYLE

I promise. It will be just like the one Philainis wears. But listen: I want to teach you how you should conduct yourself with men. Take my words to heart, daughter. We have only your favor with men to depend on for a living.

You can't imagine how hard it has been for us to get along since your blessed father's death. We lacked nothing when he was alive. He had quite a reputation as a blacksmith in the Piræus. People say there will never be another blacksmith like Philipinos. After his death I sold his tongs, anvil and hammer for two hundred drachmas. We lived on that for some time. I found work weaving and turning thread, barely earning enough to buy bread with. I have raised you, however, my precious little daughter. You are the only hope left me.

CORINNA

Weren't you going to say something about my hundred drachmas, mother?

CROBYLE

No, child. But I thought you were now big enough to support your tired mother. Not only that: you can even earn enough to dress richly, to buy yourself the newest robes of purple, and slaves.

CORINNA

What do you mean, mother? Why do you say that?

CROBYLE

Don't you understand, little fool? Why, you will earn a great deal being attentive to nice young men, drinking in their company and going to bed with them—for money, of course.

CORINNA (*Scandalized*)

You mean like Lyra, the daughter of Daphnis?

CROBYLE

Yes.

CORINNA

But she is—a courtesan!

CROBYLE

What of it? There is no harm in that. You will become rich. You are sure to have many lovers.

CORINNA (*Weeps*)

CROBYLE

Why, Corinna! Why do you weep? Don't you see how many courtesans there are, how they are all sought after, and how they all make money? I knew Daphnis when she was in rags—that was before she got sense enough to make use of her body. Look at her now! She struts like a queen, all bespangled with gold, wearing flowery dresses, and no less than four slaves behind her.

CORINNA

And how did she get all that, dear mother?

CROBYLE

Well, in the first place, by dressing elegantly and being amiable and cheery with everybody. She does not giggle at any little thing, as you do; instead, she only smiles, which is much more attractive. She treats shrewdly, but without double-crossing, the men that come to see her or take her to their houses. She never approaches them first. When she is paid to assist at a banquet, she takes care not to get drunk—it is foolish and men can't bear it—and she does not stuff herself with food like an imbecile, so that when she gets into bed she is in condition to serve her lover well. She no more than touches the various dishes served—delicately, with her fingertips, and always in silence. And she never guzzles her wine, but drinks slowly, quietly, in gentle little sips.

CORINNA

But supposing she is thirsty, dear mother?

CROBYLE

Especially when she is thirsty, foolish girl! And she never speaks more than is necessary, and never pokes fun at anybody present, and has eyes only for the man who has paid her. That is why everybody appreciates her. Furthermore, when it is time to get into bed, she never resorts to any obscenity, but does her task with care and loving attention. In bed, she bears one thing in mind—to win the man and make a steady lover of him. That is why everybody speaks highly of her. If you take this lesson to heart and do likewise we, too, shall be rich, for she is far from having your looks and your complexion. But I won't say anything more. Long may you live, little daughter, and prosper!

CORINNA

But tell me, dear mother: Will all those that will pay me be as handsome as Eucritos, the fellow I slept with yesterday?

CROBYLE

Not all. There will be better looking fellows. And some will be very vigorous and energetic—you know what I mean; while others will not be quite as handsome.

CORINNA

And shall I have to give myself to the homely fellows too?

CROBYLE

Especially to them, my child. It is that class that pays best. The beautiful kind only want to give their looks. I repeat: be careful to attach yourself to men who pay best—if you want to have people point you out on the street and say: "Do you see that Corinna, the daughter of Crobyle? Do you notice how rich she became, and what happiness she brings to her old mother? Oh, thrice happy has she rendered her, blessed be the girl!"

What do you say, child? Will you do that? You'll do what your old mother tells you, won't you? Ah, you will easily surpass the best of our courtesans. Now run and wash yourself, child. Possibly little Eucritos will be back tonight. He has promised to come to my little daughter. Both of you will enjoy it more tonight.

SWEETHEART

MOUSARION, a courtesan, 18 years old
HER MOTHER

SWEETHEART

MOTHER

If you ever find another lover like Chaireas, my dear Mousarion, we shall have to sacrifice a white goat to the popular Aphrodite and a heifer to the Uranian of the Gardens, and we shall crown with flowers the kind Demeter, from whom all riches flow. For we shall be happy. Yes, thrice happy!

You should understand by now how much we are ever likely to get from that young man. He hasn't given us a single obole, or one piece of clothing or a pair of slippers, and not a box of perfumes. His only stock in trade seems to be pretexts, promises and fine hopes. He is always mumbling:

"If my father ever and—I become master of the estate, everything, everything will be yours." You say he has sworn to marry you legally?

MOUSARION

He did, mother. He swore by the two goddesses and by Athena Palleas.

MOTHER

And you believe all that? Why, the other day, when he did not have enough money to pay a debt, you handed him your ring; you said nothing to me. And he traded it for a few drinks. Then followed both of your Ionic necklaces, each of which weighs no less than two *darikes*. The armorer Praxias of Chios had to send to Ephesus to get them for you. Well, dear Chaireas had better start paying what he owes us. I won't say anything about your linen and shirts. Every lover naturally gives those things. But Chaireas isn't much of an asset as a lover.

MOUSARION

But he is so handsome. There isn't a sign of a hair on his chin. And he tells me he loves me and often weeps while he is saying that he loves me. Furthermore, he is the son of Dinomache and Lathes the Areopagite. We shall get married as soon as the old man shuts his eyes for good.

MOTHER (*Ironically*)

Well, Mousarion. Whenever we are in need of shoes and the cobbler says, "Two drachmas, please," we shall tell him, "Sorry, we have no money, but won't you take a few fine hopes?" And when the flour merchant presents his bill, we'll say, "Wait. The old Laches Collyetus will soon be dead. We shall pay after the marriage ceremony." Aren't you ashamed of yourself? You are the only one among courtesans without a pair of earrings, without a necklace, or one Tarentine tunic?

MOUSARION

Why should I feel ashamed, mother? Are the other courtesans happier or better looking?

MOTHER

But they are more intelligent. They understand their business. They don't let their heads be turned by fine phrases and promises. You are faithful; you love Chaireas like a husband, you don't let another soul touch you. That is the trouble with you. The other day, when the Acharnian farmer boy offered you two hundred drachmas, the full price of the wine he had sold for his father in the city, and the Acharnian had no hair on his chin, either, you laughed at the poor boy and lay down instead with Chaireas, your Adonis.

MOUSARION

But, mother, you surely did not expect me to abandon Chaireas and receive in his place that peasant with his smell of goats and cow-dung? Chaireas's skin is so smooth and soft. It is just like the skin of a suckling pig from Acharnai.

MOTHER

Fine. That was a rustic who smelled of goats and cow-dung. But what about Antiphon, the son of Menecrates? Why didn't you receive Antiphon? He offered you a hundred drachmas for the pleasure of one night? Isn't he handsome? Isn't he a man of the world? Isn't he citified? Is Antiphon a day older than your dear little Chaireas?

MOUSARION

But Chaireas says he will kill both of us if he ever finds him with me.

MOTHER

How those young fellows do threaten and boast! In that case, you will remain without lovers, you will become an honest woman. Why don't you forget that you are a courtesan and put on the dress of the priestesses of the Thesmophorion goddess? But let us leave that. Today is the day of Aloa, a feast of Demeter. What has your little darling given you for the holiday?

MOUSARION

Always you think and speak only of what he will give me. He gives me himself. Has any courtesan more? But—there mother, do not weep. His father has promised him a fine gift of money. Chaireas promised to give whatever stipend he receives to me. He is generous. Have no fear, dear mother.

MOTHER

Let us hope it isn't more lying. Don't you forget my words, Mousarion. I'll have occasion to remind you of your folly.

THE PLEASURE OF BEING BEATEN

CHRYSIS, 17 years old }Courtesans
AMPELIS, 35 years old

THE PLEASURE OF BEING BEATEN

AMPELIS

Why are you so sad, Chrysis? And your eyes are red with crying. I have always known you as a cheerful girl. You, of all our friends, should be happy. For it is common gossip that Gorgias loves you with a love that is bestowed on few women.

CHRYSIS

Yes, that is just it. He loves me! But you would not have thought so had you seen him last night, in that insane fury that overcomes him when I but walk in the shadow of another man. No, had you seen him beating me last night, would you but see the marks of his lash on my body now, you would not think him such a lover. Lover indeed! He whips me with more fury than the meanest slave.

AMPELIS

But this fury is only another proof of his great love. You should he thankful, not complaining.

CHRYSIS

What are you saying? Must he always be beating me?

AMPELIS

No. But may he always get angry when your attention wanders to some other man! He must be crazy about you. If he weren't, he wouldn't have gotten excited when he saw you with another lover.

CHRYSIS

But I have no other lover. He imagines that I am in love with a rich old man just because I spoke to the fellow the other day.

AMPELIS

It is a very good thing that he thinks the rich are after you. The more he will suffer on account of that, the more he will try to rival them—you know how—so as not to be left behind.

CHRYSIS

Meanwhile, he raises Cain and whips me and gives me not an obole.

AMPELIS

He'll give. Jealous men are always liberal givers.

CHRYSIS

But, dearie, I don't see why he should keep on beating me.

AMPELIS

I am not saying that. I do know, however, that men become bigger-hearted and better lovers once they get the suspicion that their mistresses care less about them. When a man believes himself to be the one and only lover in a woman's life, he'll whistle and go his way.

I ought to know; I have followed this profession for the last twenty years. If you want me to, I will tell you what happened to me a few years ago.

At that time I had a steady lover, a certain Demophantos, a usurer living near Poikile. He had never given me more than five drachmas and he pretended to be my man. But his love was only superficial, Chrysis. He never sighed, he never shed tears for me and he never spent the night waiting at my door. One day he came to see me, knocked at my door, but I did not open it. You see, I had the painter, Callides, in my room; Callides had given me ten drachmas. Demophantos swore and beat his fists on the door and left cursing me. Several days passed without my sending for him; Callides was still in my house. Thereupon Demophantos, who was already quite excited, went wild. He broke open my door, wept, pulled me about, threatened to kill me, tore my tunic, and did everything, in fact, that a jealous man would do, and finally presented me with six thousand drachmas. In consideration of this sum, I was his for a period of eight months. His wife used to say that I had bewitched him with some powder. That bewitching powder, to be sure, was jealousy. That is why, Chrysis, I advise you to act likewise with Gorgias. The boy will be rich if anything happens to his father.

THE MISTAKE

JOESSA, a courtesan
PYTHIAS, her courtesan friend
LYSIAS, an Athenian youth in love with Joessa

THE MISTAKE

JOESSA

You forget how I have treated you, Lysias. Never have I asked you for money. Never have I left you at my door, saying, "There is another man inside." And I have never obliged you to exploit your father or to fool your mother in order to procure clothing and gifts for me, as other courtesans are always doing. You know what fine lovers I have slighted for your sake. There was Etocles, who is now a prytanian, and Pasion, the armorer, and your own comrade, Melissos, whose father is dead, so that he can make full use of the entire family estate. You, only you, have ever been my Phaon. I had eyes only for you. After the first day of our acquaintance I did not let anybody but you enter my bed.

Ah, I was foolish enough to place faith in our vows; yes, as wise as Penelope, though my mother shouted at me and complained to all my friends. And you, Lysias, now that you know that I am entirely yours and am dying for your love, you play with the body of Lykaine in my presence and praise Magidion, the cithara player, when I embrace you at night in bed. You hurt me. Your actions bring tears to my eyes. I feel outraged. The other day you drank with Thrason and Diphilos.

25

Kymbalion, the flute player, and Pyrallis, who is my enemy, you know, were there too. I did not mind the five kisses you gave Kymbalion. It was yourself you had insulted when you kissed that woman. But what nasty signs you made to Pyrallis! And when you drank wine, you sent her your cup, whispering to the slave not to hand it to anybody else if Pyrallis did not wish to drink. And later you bit an apple, and seeing Diphilos occupied elsewhere, you threw the bitten apple into the lap of that Pyrallis. And she kissed it and slipped the apple between her breasts.

Why do you do all these things? Have I ever been unkind to you? Do I ever as much as glance at any other man? Do I not live for you alone? (*She weeps.*) You are not just, Lysias. You torture a woman whose only misfortune is to be in love with you. But there is a goddess, the kind Adrasteia, who notices such things. Possibly you, yourself, will weep very soon when you find out that I have strangled myself in my bed or thrown myself down a well. You will feel as triumphant as if you had managed some great feat.

Why do you regard me with angry eyes and gnash your teeth? If you have any reproaches to make, speak out, and Pythias will judge between us. What is the matter? (*Lysias goes out.*) You leave me without a word. You see, Pythias, how much I suffer on account of my Lysias

PYTHIAS

Oh, the boor! Her tears do not touch him. You are not a man: you are a statue of stone. (*To Joessa.*) I must say that you are partly responsible for this situation. You have spoilt him. He did not deserve so much attention. Men despise women who love too much and unwisely. Do not weep, dearie! Take my advice. Shut your door in his face. You will see how enthusiastic he will become about his Joessa after passing the night at your door in the street.

JOESSA

Ah, do not offer me such advice. I shall never be so cruel to Lysias.

LYSIAS (*Without having heard*)

I haven't returned because of your friend, Pythias. I refuse to look at this woman again. I have turned back in order to speak to you. You have no bad thoughts about me. You do not say that Lysias is a bad fellow.

PYTHIAS

Indeed, I have just said something to that effect.

LYSIAS (*Loud*)

So you want me to remain silent and do nothing while this Joessa fools me with other men? Yes, the other day I found her in bed with a young man!

PYTHIAS (*Not surprised*)

After all, she is a courtesan, Lysias. Going to bed with young men is, as I may put it, her occupation. However, when was it you found the strange young man in Joessa's bed?

LYSIAS

About five days ago. Yes, by Dzeus, it was five days ago. Today is the seventh day of the month and that was the second. Having discovered I was the lover of this virtuous maiden, my father shut me up in the house, ordering the porter not to let me out. But not being able to endure separation from her, I ordered Dromon to let himself down the court wall, which is quite low, and when he got over the court wall, I lowered myself onto his shoulders and got out without more difficulty. But why annoy you with so many words? I escaped; I came here; I found the door carefully shut. It was about midnight when I reached the street. I did not knock on the door, but lifted it quietly off its hinges; I had done this once before. I entered without a sound. Groping my way along the wall, I arrived at Joessa's bed.

JOESSA (*Aside*)

What is he saying, O Demeter? I am in agony.

LYSIAS

Well, once near her bed, I became aware of two breathing peacefully in the dark of the night. At first, I thought Lyde was sleeping with Joessa; but touching the other person lightly with my hand, I felt a smooth face, not that of an aged woman. The face was without a hair. And the head—hear, kind Pythias—the head was heavily perfumed and—shaven! A man's head. The young man was comfortably couched. He reclined between Joessa's legs, apparently she was to hold him in a long embrace the entire night. Ah, if I had had a sword, I would have ended the play there and then! Why do you laugh? Is there anything ludicrous about such perfidy?

JOESSA

So it was no more than this that hurt your feelings, Lysias? Why, it was Pythias who was in bed with me.

PYTHIAS (*Ashamed*)

Please, Joessa, don't tell him JOESSA

Why shouldn't I tell him? I assure you it was Pythias, my dear, I asked her to sleep with me that night. I was sad and lonely without you.

LYSIAS

Oh, yes! Pythias was a young man with a shaved head. How thick and long has her hair grown within the last six days!

JOESSA

No, Lysias. She has had her hair cut and her head shaved since a recent sickness. Her hair started to fall out. Show him, Pythias. Show him, Pythias Show him your head. (*Pythias takes off the wig.*) Here is the adulterous ephebus who excited your jealousy.

LYSIAS

Shouldn't I have been jealous, Joessa? Do you blame me? I couldn't help it. I was in love and I hac touched her shaven head.

JOESSA

But now you are fully convinced? It is my turn to be angry.

LYSIAS

No, dear Joessa. Let us not be angry. We shall go out and find some drink. Come with us, Pythias. It is fitting that you take part in our peace libations.

JOESSA

She will come along. Oh, how much I have suffered on your account, Pythias, you dearest of young lovers!

PYTHIAS

But everything is all right, now, isn't it? Therefore, bear no grudge against your Pythias. And please, I beg you not to tell anybody about my wig.

THE INCANTATION

BACCHIS } Courtesans
MELITTA

THE INCANTATION

MELITTA

If you happen to know of a witch, I refer to those Thessalonian women who practice incantations, by which they win love for the most detestable of women, send her to me. I will give all my clothes, all my gold, everything I own, to see Charinos hate Simiche and return to me.

BACCHIS

What is it you're saying? Is he no longer with you? Is it possible that Charinos, is in love with Simiche? He has suffered so many quarrels with his parents on account of you. He has thrown over that rich fiancée of his and her dowry of five talents for Melitta.

MELITTA

Ah, all that belongs to the past. I haven't seen him for the last five days. Charinos has deserted me. He and Simiche are drinking at the house of his friend Ramænes.

BACCHIS

That is terrible, Melitta. But how did you happen to fall out? Undoubtedly it was not over a trifle.

MELITTA

I have nothing to say about that. The day before yesterday he returned from the Piræus where he went to collect a debt for his father. I ran up to him as he entered my house, but he refused to recognize me. I wanted to embrace him but he repelled me, saying:

"Get away from me! Run along to your armorer Hermotimos! Or rather, see what is written on the Keramic walls; you'll find there both of your names inscribed with a stylus."

"Which Hermotimos?" I asked him in surprise.

But without answering and without tasting a morsel of food, he got into bed and turned his back on me. I did everything I could think of to win his attention. I took him in my arms, I lay on top of him, I kissed him between the shoulders, on the lower section of his back, and put my hand between his legs. It was all in vain. Nothing could soften him, and he said:

"If you continue your maneuvers, I'll leave immediately, dark and late as it is!"

BACCHIS

But you do know Hermotimos, don't you?

MELITTA

May I become even more miserable than I am at present if I know of an armorer by the name of Hermotimos. Charinos rose at daybreak and left without a word. I remembered what he had said about the Keramic wall and I sent Akis to see what was written. She found nothing more than an inscription, somewhere on the right, as you enter by the *dipylos*. It went like this: "Melitta loves Hermotimos"; and a little lower: "The armorer Hermotimos loves Melitta."

BACCHIS

What a dirty trick! I understand now. Somebody wrote the words on the wall in order to get even with Charinos, knowing he is very jealous. He believed what he read without asking a question. If I saw him, I'd tell him about it.

MELITTA

But how can you see him? How can anybody see him? He has shut himself up with Simiche. His parents came to my house to see if Charinos was with me. Ah, if only I could find an old witch who would make the right kind of incantation. She'd save my life.

BACCHIS

Don't worry, my dear. I happen to be acquainted with an experienced witch. She is a Syrian, still in the prime of her career as a magician. You remember how Phanias left me for no reason at all, just like Charinos now? Well, this Syrian witch worked a reconciliation after four months' time. I was despairing of ever getting him back, and she, by the means of her enchantments, made him return to my bed.

MELITTA

What did the old woman do—if you do not fear telling me?

BACCHIS

Not at all. I'll tell you everything. You don't need to pay her very much, Melitta, only one drachma and a loaf of bread. But you will have to bring along some salt, seven oboles, sulfur and a torch. The witch takes it all, and—oh, yes! You must bring some wine in a krater; the old woman will drink the wine. And you'll need something of the man himself as, for example, an article of clothing, a hair, or some such thing.

MELITTA

I still have his shoes.

BACCHIS

Well, she will hang them on a nail, burn the sulfur underneath and strew salt over the fire while she keeps repeating your name, your own and your lover's. Then she draws a top from between her breasts and spins it, reciting at the same time her secret charm. Oh, what secret, barbarian words! It'll make you shudder.

That is what she did for me, and very soon Phanias—in spite of the reproaches of his comrades and the pleading of the false Phoibis—came back to my bed. It was the charm that made him return. It urged him on toward me.

The same witch also taught me the way to make Phoibis perfectly hateful. You watch the print of her feet as she passes by, and then you rub out the footprints by putting your right foot where she has placed her left foot and your left on her right. You do it and say at the same time: "I have trampled on you; I am above you. I am above you. I have trampled on you; I am above you."

I did exactly what she told me, and now Phanias is back in my bed. And he passionately kisses me all over my body, something he always refused to do before.

MELITTA

Not a moment's delay, Bacchis! Find me immediately the Syrian witch. And you, Akis, prepare the bread and the sulfur and everything we shall need for a proper incantation.

THE TERROR OF MARRIAGE

MYRTION, a young courtesan
PAMPHILOS, her boy lover
DORIS, her slave

THE TERROR OF MARRIAGE

MYRTION

You are going to marry the daughter of Pheidon, the pilot. Possibly you have already married her. All your vows, all your tears, all your promises, have gone the way of smoke. You have forgotten Myrtion, now that I am in a family way—it is the eighth month. Yes, a big belly is all that is left me from your great love. Pretty soon I shall have to feed an infant, a fine job for a courtesan. For I will never destroy what I shall have brought forth, especially if it is a man-child. I shall name the child Pamphilos and keep him as my consolation. And one day your son will face you and reproach you for having deserted his unfortunate mother.

I know it is not a beautiful girl you have chosen as your wife. I saw her recently at the Thesmophorion games. She was with her mother. I did not think at that time I should lose my Pamphilos on account of such a creature. Why don't you inspect her more closely? Examine her face and her eyes. One of these days you might be sorry to have married a woman whose eyes squint. Indeed, they are like a fish's.

But you have seen Pheidon, your fiancée's father. Well, all one needs is to take a good look at his face; there is no need of seeing his daughter after that.

PAMPHILOS

But you are talking nonsense, Myrtion. How long must I hear you talk about pilots' daughters and marriages? Do I know if the bride in question is squint-eyed, snub-nosed or beautiful, or if Pheidon, the Alopekethian, (for it is of him you are talking, I believe) has an ugly daughter? He isn't even a friend of my father's. I recall they had a lawsuit recently over some matter of navigation. I think he owed my father one talent and refused to pay; so that my father hailed him before the maritime court. He had a hard time making the pilot yield; Pheidon never paid the entire sum.

If I wanted to get married, would I have refused the hand of the daughter of Demea who was *strategus* last year (she is my first cousin on my mother's side) in order to marry the daughter of Pheidon, the pilot? Where have you garnered such queer news? Are these chimeras the inventions of your jealousy?

MYRTION

In that case it is not true you are getting married?

PAMPHILOS

You are either crazy or drunk, Myrtion. And strange to say, we had little to drink last night.

MYRTION (*Pointing at her slave*)

It is Doris who has worried me with such ideas. I sent her to buy some strips of wool for my belly and to make an offering to the Lokheia in my behalf, and she said she met Lesbia, and Lesbia—Tell it yourself, Doris. Tell him what you have heard and seen. You are sure you haven't made up the story?

DORIS

May I be run over and crushed by a chariot, if I have told a lie! I never lie. When I was near the Prytaneion I bumped into Lesbia and she stopped me and said with a smile:

"I hear your mistress' fine lover, Pamphilos, is getting married. He is going to marry the daughter of Pheidon."

When I refused to believe it, she advised me to run down the street, Pamphilos's street, and I would surely see garlands and flute players and hear people singing the hymeneal chant.

MYRTION

And did you go to see?

DORIS

Certainly. And I found everything Lesbia mentioned.

PAMPHILOS

Now I understand your mistake. Lesbia did not actually fool you, Doris, and you have without doubt imparted the truth to my Myrtion. However, both of you permitted yourselves to become excited about nothing at all. The marriage feast you are talking about is not being celebrated in our house. I remember now that last night, upon my return home from your side, dear Myrtion, my mother happened to remark:

"Pamphilos, your friend Charmides, the son of our neighbor Aristainetos, is getting married to a good girl; he has curbed his wild desires and become respectable. Till when, son, will you continue with your shameful courtesans?"

I paid no attention to what my mother had to say. Those old folks will never understand. I went to bed. I left my home at sunrise this morning, so that I noticed absolutely nothing of what Doris was to see later. If you don't believe me, Doris, return and examine with care, not only the street, but also the door. You will see which door is decorated with garlands.

MYRTION

You have saved my life, Pamphilos. I would have strangled myself.

PAMPHILOS

It will never, never happen. I am not so foolish. I will never forget my Myrtion, especially when she carries a child of mine in her belly. How I would like to lie with you now! You are even more beautiful with your belly bulging big. Oh, Myrtion, let me!

MYRTION

Have me, dear Pamphilos! But lean lightly.

THE LESBIANS

LEAINA, a player of the cithara
CLONARION, a young man

THE LESBIANS

CLONARION

I have heard a queer thing said about you, Leaina. People say Megilla, the wealthy lady from Lesbos, is in love with you, as if she were a man, and that she—I can't explain how—but—. I have heard it said that the two of you couple up just like—

LEAINA (*Abashed silence*)

CLONARION

What's the matter? You are blushing. Is it true then?

LEAINA

It is true, Clonarion. I am ashamed. It is so strange—

CLONARION

By the great Adrasteia, you must tell me about it! What does that woman require of you? Exactly what do you do when you get into bed together?

LEAINA (*Abashed silence*)

CLONARION

Now I am sure you don't love me. If you did, you would not think of hiding such things from me.

LEAINA

I do love you, Clonarion. I love you more than anybody else. But this is such a strange matter. I am so ashamed. That woman is so terribly like a male.

CLONARION

I don't understand. Do you mean to say she is one of those man-like females of Lesbos who will not suffer in their beds the company of men, but prefer to find pleasure, instead, with other women, as if they themselves were men?

LEAINA

She is somewhat like that.

CLONARION (*With enthusiasm*)

In that case, Leaina, tell me everything, please! How did she seduce you, in the first place? And how was it that you let Megilla have her way with you? And what came after? Tell me everything, please!

LEAINA

You see, Megilla and Demonassa, the Corinthian, sweating and very hot, pulled off her false hair—I had never suspected her of wearing a wig. And I saw her

head was smooth-shaven as that of a young athlete. I was quite scared to see this. But Megilla spoke up and said to me:

"Tell me, O Leaina, have you ever seen a better looking young man?"

"But I see no young man here, Megilla!" I told her.

"Now, now! Don't you effeminate me!" she reproved. "You must understand my name is Megillos. Demonassa is my wife."

Her words seemed so funny to me, Clonarion. I started to giggle. And I said:

"Can it be, Megillos, that you are a man and lived among us under the disguise of a woman, just like Achilles, who stayed among the girls hidden by his purple robe? And is it true that you possess a man's organs, and that you do to Demonassa what any husband does to his wife?"

"That Leaina," she replied, "is not entirely so. You will soon see how we shall couple up in a fashion that is much more voluptuous."

"In that case," I said, "you are not a hermaphrodite. They, I have been told, have both a man's and woman's organs."

"No," she said, "I am quite like a man."

"Ismenodora, the Boietian flute player, has told me about a Theban woman who was changed into a man. A certain good soothsayer by the name of Teiresias— Did any accident like that happen to you by chance?"

"No, Leaina," she said. "I was born with a body entirely like that of all women, but I have the tastes and desires of a man."

"And do those desires of yours suffice you?" I asked, smiling.

"Let me have my own way with you, Leaina, if you don't believe me," she answered, "and you will soon see that I have nothing to envy men for. I have something that resembles a man's estate. Come on, let me do what I want to do and you will soon understand."

She pleaded so hard that I let her have her way. And you must understand that she made me a gift of a splendid necklace and several tunics of the finest linen. Then I embraced her and held her in my arms, as if she wire a man. And she kissed me all over the body, and she set out to do what she had promised, panting excitedly from the great pleasure and desire that possessed her.

CLONARION

But exactly how did she manage it? What did she do? Tell me, Leaina! Tell me especially that!

LEAINA

Please, don't ask me for details. These are shameful things. By the Mistress of Heaven, I will never, never, tell you that!

THE RETURN OF THE SOLDIER

PANNYCHIS, a courtesan
POLEMON, her former lover
PHILOSTRATOS, her new lover
DORCAS, her slave

THE RETURN OF THE SOLDIER

DORCAS (*Runs in*)

Oh, mistress, we are lost! We are lost! Polemon is back from the war. He was wearing a purple cloak and was surrounded by many slaves. I did not get the opportunity to speak to him in person because, as soon as they caught sight of him, his friends rushed up to greet him. But I noticed at his side a person who had accompanied him abroad; you know whom I mean. And I asked the latter person:

"Tell me, Parmenon, have you got something for us? Has your master brought any worth-while gift from the war?"

PANNYCHIS

That was wrong. You shouldn't have used such words. You should have said instead: "You are safe, praised be the gods, especially Dzeus Xenios and Athena Stratia! The mistress has asked me to inquire how your master has gotten along and if both of you are in good health."

And it would have sounded even better if you had added: "She hasn't ceased weeping for Polemon and thinking about him." That would have been much better.

DORCAS

Indeed, I did tell something like what you say as soon as I opened my mouth. But I didn't repeat my words, the exact words I used to Parmenon, because I wanted to warn you immediately what I have learned. When I came near Parmenon, I started this way:

"Is it possible, Parmenon, that your own and your master's ears did not tingle all thru this war? For the mistress hasn't stopped talking about both of you. She has shed tears every day since you left. And whenever anybody returns from the battle area and there is news of a great fight and many are killed, she tears her hair and beats her breasts. Indeed, any kind of war news makes her lament."

PANNYCHIS

Very good, Dorcas. You have spoken the right words.

DORCAS

Then I asked about gifts and such matters, and he replied: "Dorcas, we return in full magnificence."

PANNYCHIS

He did not begin by saying that Polemon still remembers me and that he hopes to find me alive and awaiting him?

DORCAS

In fact, Parmenon did mention several little things to that effect; but I found much more agreeable his account of his master's and his own good fortune. Parmenon spoke at length of great riches, of gold, fine raiments and slaves and ivory. It appears that they have so much money that they don't count it by pieces but by *medimnas*, and many are the *medimnas* they have brought along. Parmenon himself carries on his little finger a large polygonal ring in which is set a wonderful tri-colored stone.

Before I left him, he tried to tell me how they had crossed the Halys and killed a certain Tiridates, and how Polemon distinguished himself in a fight against the Pisidians. I ran to you to announce their return so that you may have time to decide what to do. Should Polemon arrive and find Philostratos here, he will—Can you imagine what he might do?

PANNYCHIS

We must find some remedy for this queer situation. It would not be wise to desert Philostratos; he gave me six thousand drachmas the other day. And, besides, he is a merchant; he may give me much more later. On the other hand, I can not refuse to receive Polemon when he returns with so much money. One must respect old loves. This Polemon is so jealous a man, it was hard to put up with him when he was poor. I can imagine what he will be like after such a successful war.

DORCAS

Here he comes!

PANNYCHIS

Oh, I am powerless! What shall I do? I can not think of a way out. Invent something, please. Invent a story immediately! I tremble, Dorcas! I tremble!

DORCAS

And there is Philostratos, too!

PANNYCHIS

Oh, what will become of me! May the earth open its mouth and swallow me

PHILOSTRATOS (*Coming near*)

I suggest we have a drink, dear Pannychis.

PANNYCHIS

(*Low*) Oh, miserable man, you have ruined me! (*Loudly*) Hail, Polemon! Why didn't you return sooner?

POLEMON

Who is the man who dares to ask Pannychis to drink with him?

PANNYCHIS (*Silent*)

POLEMON

You are silent. Very well. I have exerted myself to make the journey from Thermopylae to this city in five days' time in order to see this woman! Many thanks! I must have merited such a reception. From now on you are free to sponge on somebody else.

PHILOSTRATOS

And you, friend, who are you?

POLEMON

What! You haven't heard of Polemon of Steirieus, the Pandionide who was first a chiliarch and now commands his five thousand shields? Polemon, stranger, was the lover of this Pannychis when he still credited her with human feelings.

PHILOSTRATOS

All right, my captain of mercenaries! Learn that Pannychis is mine. She has already received from me six thousand drachmas and will get more as soon as I sell my cargo. Come along, Pannychis. Let our valiant chiliarch disport himself with the Odrysians.

DORCAS

My mistress is free. She will follow whomever she pleases

PANNYCHIS (*Low*)

What shall I do, Dorcas?

DORCAS

It is best to return inside. You can't remain near Polemon while he is in such a dudgeon. He will become even more jealous.

PANNYCHIS

All right. Let us go in.

POLEMON

I warn you that this is the last time you will drink together. It is not for play alone that I have survived so many a martial slaughter. I shall kill. My Thracians, Parmenon! Let the phalanx cut off this street from the rest of the metropolis! To the front, hoplites! Slingers and bowmen on the flanks! The rest to the rear of the column!

PHILOSTRATOS

You think you are talking to children, mercenary. Do you believe you frighten us? Ah, what grand words! Indeed, have you ever killed a rooster? Where did you see war? You may have mounted guard over some safe rampart; possibly not even that.

POLEMON

You will learn very soon where I saw war. Wait till you see us in arms!

PHILOSTRATOS

Come on then! Bring on your phalanx! I and this faithful Tibios will show you what can be done with stones and oyster shells. We'll make you run so hard that you won't know the why or whither of your hurry.

THE LITTLE FLUTE PLAYER

COCHLIS, a courtesan
PARTHENIS, a flute player

THE LITTLE FLUTE PLAYER

COCHLIS

Why the tears, Parthenis? Where do you hail from with your flutes all broken?

PARTHENIS

The soldier, the Aitolian, the big fellow, he beat me because he found me playing in the house of that Crocale woman. I was paid by Gorgos. Gorgos is his rival. And he broke my flutes and beat me and did all kinds of nasty things. And he turned over the table and threw himself on the *krater* and emptied it. And then he seized Gorgos, the farmer, by his hair and dragged him out of the banquet hall. And the soldier—I think Deinomachos is his name—and some of his comrades surrounded the farmer and beat him so hard. I don't know, Cochlis, if he'll ever recover. Blood flowed from his nostrils and his face was swollen and blue.

COCHLIS

Was the man insane or drunk? It sounds like the work of a drunkard.

PARTHENIS

I think it was jealousy, Cochlis, jealousy and too much love. Crocale asked the soldier for twelve hundred drachmas if he wanted to have her exclusively for himself. Deinomachos refused to give the sum, and she shut the door in his face and received instead Gorgos of Oinoe, a rich farmer who had been in love with her for some time. They drank together and I came to play the flute.

The banquet was going along fine. I had just finished a Lydian melody and the farmer had got up and danced, while the Crocale beat time with her palms, and everything was joyful, when all of a sudden there was a noise and a shout and the front door burst off its hinges and eight young men rushed into the hall, the Megarian among them. Without stopping to explain, they overturned the table; and Gorgos, as I have said, was knocked down, kicked and beaten on his head. The Crocale woman succeeded in saving herself by running away to the house of her neighbor, the courtesan Thespias.

As for me, Deinomachos slapped me good and hard and called me "Ball of Smut" and threw my flutes in my face. Then two of his soldier friends tore my

robe and tunic off my body and played with me. They slapped and beat
me about my thighs till my nether part was burning red. Then they lifted
their own tunics and made me sink down in their laps so that I felt very
much ashamed. Then they obliged me to take . . . . . between my lips,
saying: "Try a new melody, genial little flute player!"

Now I am bound for my master's house. I am going to tell him
everything that happened. The farmer went to find friends in the city to
help him bring the Megarian to justice.

COCHLIS

That is what you get out of those resplendent military love affairs—blows and lawsuits. To hear them talk they are all chiliarchs or hegemons. But when it comes to paying for services rendered—"Wait," they say, "Wait till I get paid. As soon as I receive my salary, you will surely be made happy."

Let those boasters carry themselves off to their wars! May they all be killed off! I believe I do best by not receiving any of that herd. All others are welcome: fishermen, sailors, farmers, they are all welcome. They don't know how to flatter, but they pay. Anyhow, those flaunters of plumes and tellers of martial tales are never serious lovers. What do they know about love!

THERE IS A TIME FOR LYING

LEONTICHOS, an affectionate soldier
CHENIDAS, his comrade-in-arms
HYMNIS, an innocent young courtesan

THERE IS A TIME FOR LYING

LEONTICHOS (*Bombastically*)

And what about the battle with the Galateans, Chenidas? Do you remember how I rode my white charger ahead of all our horsemen and how the Galateans, who are pretty brave fellows at that, trembled as soon as they saw me, so that not a warrior among them dared to face me. And then, throwing my javelin, I pierced their hipparchos and his mount. As for those that reassembled—for after their phalanx was broken, some Galateans reorganized as a square—I attacked them sword in hand. The sudden burst forward of my faithful steed knocked over the first seven. With a swing of my blade I hacked in halves the head of their chief. Our men then came up, but the enemy was already in flight.

CHENIDAS

And do you recall Paphlagonia, Leontichos? You did grand work in that country too. Do you remember how, single-handed, you engaged the Satrap himself?

LEONTICHOS

Thanks for reminding me of the event. The Satrap, you know, had the build of a giant. He was reputed to be an extraordinary swordsman, and held us Greeks in contempt. Now one afternoon he rode forward between the two armies and shouted: "Who wants to brave a fight with me?"

Fright seized our men. The lochages, the taxiarchs, and even our hegemon, who is far from cowardly (it was Aristachmos the Aitolian who commanded us then; he is handy with the javelin), all were rather nervous about the challenge. At that time I wasn't even a chiliarch. But in a spontaneous fit of recklessness, pushing away those among my friends who tried to hold me back (for they had their doubts as to my safety, the barbarian Hercules seemed so formidable in his gilded armor, as he stood before our army shaking his huge plumed head and brandishing his enormous javelin), I—I—

CHENIDAS

I confess that I myself was among those who were worried about your safety, Leontichos. You remember how I tried to detain you, pleading with my beloved Leontichos not to sacrifice himself for our sake. Many of our Greeks would have found life unbearable without the comradeship of the brave Leontichos.

LEONTICHOS

But I, in a reckless burst to the fore, I advanced towards the haughty enemy. I was as well armed as the Paphlagonian; I, too, was harnessed in gold. Upon my appearance in view of all, a cry arose from both armies, for I was recognized, especially by my shield, my martial ornaments and helmet plume. Let us hear a word, Chenidas! Tell us now, whom did everybody compare me with?

CHENIDAS

By Dzeus, whom could we have compared you with at that moment, if not to Achilles, the son of Thetis and Peleus? How well your helmet suited you! And the purple of your cloak shone like—my, I can't think of what! Your shield made bolts of lightning in the air.

LEONTICHOS

And when we met—well, the barbarian was the first to draw blood. Oh! he scratched me a bit, below the knee, you know. But I—one well aimed blow and my reliable sarissee tore thru his heavy shield and wounded him in the chest. He fell at my feet, more from surprise than weakness. Then I stood on his body for a while. There was only one thing to do. Drawing my sword, I cut off the Satrap's head. Well, I gathered his collection of arms and returned to our side with the giant's head stuck on the spike of my sarissee. Blood from the disseevered head dripped on my own. You can imagine the applause that greeted me upon my return.

HYMNIS (*Nauseated*)

Ah, go away, you sickening Leontichos! What disgusting stories you tell!;: Who could look at you, least of all applaud you, after that bloody mess? Do you believe I could force myself to sleep with you after your tales of killing and blood? I am going away.

LEONTICHOS

Please don't go. I'll pay you doubly; but don't go away.

HYMNIS

I can not go to bed with an assassin.

LEONTICHOS

Don't be afraid of me, Hymnis. All that happened in the country of the Paphlagonians. I am at peace right now.

HYMNIS

No, I don't want you. You are an abominable man. From the barbarian's head stuck on your sarissee blood dripped down on your own head. And you expect me to take an odious man like you in my arms and kiss you! By the Charites, never, never will I kiss you! A man like you is no better than an executioner.

LEONTICHOS

Ah, if you could see me in arms! I am sure you would fall in love with Leontichos.

HYMNIS

Why, only hearing your cruel tales is enough to make me feel sick at heart and hate you. I imagine seeing shadows about us; these must be the phantoms of your victims. Surely the poor chief whose head you had split in two is among them. And how I would feel if I saw the fight and the blood and the corpses stretched in the mud! I believe I'd die. I could never bear to see the smallest animal killed.

LEONTICHOS

What a dear little coward you are, Hymnis! I thought you would find my story amusing.

HYMNIS

Go and tell such stories to the Lemnians or the fifty daughters of Danais, if you find any. They will find them amusing. I will sleep in my mother's house tonight. Follow me, Grammis. Take good care of yourself this night, valiant chiliarch! And do not kill too many! (*She leaves.*)

LEONTICHOS

Stay, O Hymnis, stay!—Oh, she is gone!

CHENIDAS

It is your own fault, Leontichos. You have scared the child with your cock-and-bull stories. I saw her turn yellow when you started your tale about the captain. And her eyes stood out and she shivered when you described how you cut off the Satrap's head.

LEONTICHOS

I thought she'd like me the more. But it was you who lost me altogether by putting in my head the idea of the duel.

CHENIDAS

I wanted to help you. But it was you, yourself, who made the story too horrible for the girl's tastes. You could have had your dirty Paphlagonian head without having it stuck on the end of a sarissee and without smearing yourself with the Satrap's blood.

LEONTICHOS

It is true. My story was a bit too strong for the likes of Hymnis. The rest, however, wasn't so badly imagined. Won't you help an old comrade in trouble, Chenidas? Please run after her. Persuade her to go to bed with me after all.

CHENIDAS

I'll tell her that you have invented those war stories in order to appear brave in her eyes.

LEONTICHOS

That would be too shameful, Chenidas.

CHENIDAS

Otherwise, I am sure, she will not return. I am afraid, my friend, that you must choose either to pass for a brave man and be hated, or to confess that you have lied beautifully and sleep tonight with pretty Hymnis. And by Aphrodite and Uranian, she is worth the shame of confession! The girl has a body like the dream of a well-fed soldier. Little, hard breasts like apples! Soft, resilient thighs that could unman the most gigantic of Satraps! And those dimples! Ah, Mother of Heaven, those dimples! The girl told you, Leontichos, before you started on your stories, of course, that she had a third dimple that was much more attractive. A third dimple! Ah, a third dimple! Oh, comrade, I know you will either humble yourself this evening or pass a sleepless night. I, myself, am to see Ampelis, who is, to all appearances, twice the age of the little Aphrodite whom my Mars has just scared away.

LEONTICHOS (*Very embarrassed*)

You are right. I must choose. But either alternative is hard on a fellow. However, my hand is for the sword. I prefer Hymnis. Run, therefore, Chenidas, and tell her that Leontichos has lied a little. Yes, tell her I have lied—but not altogether.

AT NIGHT

TYPHAINA, a courtesan
CHARMIDES, a lover

AT NIGHT

TYPHAINA

To hire a courtesan, pay her five drachmas, go to bed with her and then turn your back on her and weep and groan—that is a dirty trick to play on a woman with feelings. You found no pleasure in the wine at the banquet table and you were the only one not to eat. You were shedding tears; I could see that. And now you keep on sobbing like a whipped infant. Why all the humidity, Charmides? Don't hide anything from me! I'll at least carry away a bit of information from the one charming night I shall ever have passed at your manly side. I am sure I shall pass it without a wink of sleep and without

CHARMIDES

May Eros destroy me, Typhaina! I can no longer resist him. Eros is so cruel.

TYPHAINA

It isn't me that you love—that much is certain. I am but three inches away from you. We are both stark naked. And you don't seem to get excited over the fact. You repel me when I want to take you in my arms. Why, you have even dragged your clothes into bed and put the bundle as a dike between us, lest my fine emotions flow over and get you wet. Tell me: Who is the lady? Possibly I can help you. I am good at such little services.

CHARMIDES

Oh, you know her, and I think she knows you too. She is not an obscure courtesan, you understand.

TYPHAINA

Her name, Charmides?

CHARMIDES

It is Philemation, Typhaina.

TYPHAINA

Which? There are two of them, you know. Is it that girl from the Piræus who has just lost her maidenhead and is at present the mistress of Damyllos, the son of the Strategus? Or is it the woman that people have nicknamed "Pagis, the Snare"?

CHARMIDES

The latter. Hers is the bad genius that has captured me. I am obsessed by a passion for Pagis.

TYPHAINA

By Aphrodite! I wouldn't have come if I had known you called me in order to get even with that carcass of a Philemation. And now the cock has crowed thrice. I shall go my way.

CHARMIDES

Not so fast, Typhaina. If what you say of Philemation is true, I refer to the wig, her complexion and those queer spots, I can no longer bear to look at her.

TYPHAINA

Ask your mother. She might have seen her at the baths. As for her age, your grandfather, if he is still alive, will provide you with correct information.

CHARMIDES

In that case, there is little need of the dike you have joked about. Wait. I'll get my clothes out of the bed. Now, let us embrace and kiss, and we will couple up like good children. Goodbye, Philemation! My respects to your age and experience. Ah, what smooth thighs are yours, Typhaina! What joy must lie buried between them!

A POOR SAILOR'S LOVE

MYRTALE, a courtesan
DORION, her sailor friend

A POOR SAILOR'S LOVE

DORION

You have impoverished me, Myrtale, and now you won't let me in. Before, when I brought you fine gifts from abroad, you called me your beloved, your man, your master. I was your all in all. But now that I am miserably flat, and you have found for yourself a rich merchant from Bithynia, you won't let me approach you. I sit on your doorstep and shed bitter tears while he enjoys your kisses and shares your warm bed. And now you tell me you will have a child by the fat merchant. (*He weeps.*)

MYRTALE

Ah, you suffocate me, Dorion. You say that you have showered me with gifts and that I have impoverished you. How many gifts have you given me, you wet-nosed sailor? Count how many!

DORION

Very well, Myrtale, I shall count my gifts and estimate the total value of the wealth I have handed over to you, Myrtale, as proof of my love and esteem. To start with, you have those shoes from Sikyone. That's two drachmas. You won't deny that the shoes were worth two drachmas?

MYRTALE

But you slept with me for two nights.

DORION

And when I returned from Syria, I brought you an alabaster full of Phœnician perfumes. By the tail of the great god Poseidon, that amounts to another two drachmas!

MYRTALE

And what about me? Didn't I give you, before you left for the same Syria, a little tunic reaching till the thighs for you to wear while rowing? Do you remember? The proreus Epioros forgot it one day in my rooms. Yes, the proreus Epioros himself slept with me. Must I remember a poor sailor's gifts?

DORION

He took the tunic away from me, your proreus. He saw me wearing the tunic on the shore at Samos, and he took it away from me—but only after a long struggle!

And didn't I bring you a lot of onions from Cyprus and five saperdes and four perches when we returned from the Bosphorus? And when we returned from Patares, ten breads packed in one bundle and an amphora of Carian figs and a pair of sandals embroidered with gold thread? Oh, you ingrate! Dorion, the sailor, has presented you with sandals embroidered with gold. And I remember now, a huge Cythonian cheese.

MYRTALE (*Contemptuously*)

Altogether five drachmas. Five drachmas, and possibly less.

DORION (*Sadly*)

Ah, Myrtale, it was all a sailor could afford. But now I am in charge of the right flank of rowers on our ship. Why do you look at me that way? And—remember!—at the last feast of Aphrodite, I left for your account a whole drachma at the feet of the goddess. Yes, a whole silver drachma! And I gave your mother two drachmas for shoes. Very often would I leave two oboles or four in the beckoning palm of the old Lyde. All that mounts up to a fortune for a sailor.

MYRTALE

Fish and onions, Dorion.

DORION

Well, what if it is fish and onions? I can't afford more. I wouldn't find amusement at the oar of a ship if I were rich. I have never brought more than a head of garlic to my own mother. But I'd like to know what great gifts the Bithynian has ever presented you with.

MYRTALE

Do you see this robe? It was he who bought it for me. And do your fish eyes perceive this heavy necklace?

DORION

That? Why you have had it for some time!

MYRTALE

The one you saw on me before was much thinner and had no emeralds. And look at these earrings and this rug! And yesterday he gave me two hundred drachmas, and he promised to pay the rent for us. This is not sandals from Patares or cheese from Cythion and a lot of worthless chatter about love, mournful sailor!

DORION

But you don't say how he is himself. You don't describe the man you prefer to me on account of his impossible riches. He is more than fifty years old. He is bald-headed. He is as red as a lobster. And you haven't noticed his teeth, I suppose. Where are his teeth, Myrtale? I ask you: Where are his teeth? And what grace is his? O Dioscores, what grace! It is most evident when he tries to sing and play the young fellow. An ass strumming on a lyre!

You can keep your Apollo! He is quite worthy of you. May you have a son that looks like the father! As for me, I'll find my Delphis or Kymbalion. Don't you worry! Your neighbor, the flute player, looks pretty good to me. Carpets, necklaces, gifts of two hundred drachmas aren't bad. You can't have a good-looking young man like me, but you must sleep with a sack of offal, insist on carpets, necklaces and rich gifts. We can't have everything, you know.

MYRTALE (*Ironically*)

Oh, happy will be the woman whom you choose as your beloved! For you will bring her Cyprian onions and cheese upon your return from Cythion.

A MOTHER'S ADVICE

PHILINNA, a courtesan
HER WISE MOTHER

A MOTHER'S ADVICE

MOTHER

You must have been crazy yesterday, Philinna. What got into you during the banquet? Diphilos came weeping here this morning. He told me you had made him suffer. You were drunk. You rose from your couch in the middle of the meal and danced, though he had ordered you to remain at his side. After that you kissed his friend, Lamprias. And when Diphilos became angry, you left him altogether and took Lamprias in your arms and lay with him, while Diphilos choked with rage. And you did not sleep with him at night. You left Diphilos to his tears and anguish. You stretched yourself on another bed and sang all night so as to hurt him the more.

PHILINNA (*Furious*)

But he forgot to tell you what he did to me! If you knew everything, you would not be taking his side. He left me to talk to Thais, the mistress of Lamprias, who hadn't yet arrived. He saw that this made me unhappy. I beckoned for him to return to my side. Instead of coming back to me, he took hold of the tip of the lobe of Thais's ear and pulled her head backwards and gave her such a deep, sucking kiss that she could not free her lips from his for some time. I started to weep, but he only snickered and whispered all kinds of things to Thais. I am sure he was talking about me, because Thais regarded me and smiled. Then they heard Lamprias enter and they stopped kissing and separated. I went to lie down with Diphilos; I did not want to give him an excuse for further inattention.

Thais was the first to dance. She danced with her robe tucked up, so as to show her legs and thighs as if she were the only person around here having beautiful legs. When she had finished, Lamprias said not a word; but Diphilos praised as much as he could the rhythm and movement of her dance, and said: "Her foot is wedded to the cithara!" and "A beautiful leg! By Adrasteia, a beautiful leg!" And he continued with many such sayings, as if he were referring to Sosandra of Kalamis and not to that Thais whom both of us know so well. Don't we see her in the baths?

Then Thais started to mock me and said: "If somebody at this symposium is not ashamed of her spindle legs, let her get up and dance, too!

What else could I have done, mother? I got up

and danced. I wasn't going to let everybody present believe that woman was right.

MOTHER

You are too touchy, child. You shouldn't take such things to heart.

PHILINNA

Well, everybody congratulated me on my fine dancing. Diphilos, however, remained lying on his back. He kept on looking at the ceiling till I was out of breath and could dance no longer.

MOTHER

And is it true that later you kissed Lamprias and that you rose from your couch and Diphilos's side to take Lamprias in your arms? You are silent. Indeed, that is unpardonable.

PHILINNA

I wanted to render him heartache for heartache.

MOTHER

And you did not sleep with him last night! You lay on another bed and sang while he was in tears. Apparently you don't understand, my daughter, that we are poor. You forget how much we have received from Diphilos. How could we have survived the last winter if Aphrodite hadn't sent him to us.

PHILINNA

Must I then bear all kinds of insults?

MOTHER

Rage all you want, daughter, but don't ever mock any lover of yours. You don't know that men stop loving when they are laughed at. You have always been too captious with that man. Take care we do not, as the proverb says, burst the rope by pulling it too taut.

ABANDONED

GLYKERA } Courtesans
THAIS

ABANDONED

GLYKERA

By the way, Thais, do you remember the Arcanian, the soldier who used to live with Abrotonan and later fell in love with me? The fellow was always under the purple and *chlamys*. Do you know him?

THAIS

Yes, my little Glykera, I know him. He went to bed with me last year at the time of the feast of Demeter. What do you know about the man?

GLYKERA

That wicked Gorgona, who I thought was a friend of mine, played around him so shrewdly that she stole him from me.

THAIS

And now he no longer visits you? Gorgona has become his mistress, eh?

GLYKERA

Yes, Thais, and I am terribly hurt.

THAIS

That's bad, dear Glykera; but it can't be helped. Such things are to be expected among us hetairas. You ought not to worry about it and don't you speak ill of Gorgona. Abrotonan has said nothing bad about you in the same situation; you are still friends. But I wonder what that soldier sees in the woman. He must be slightly blind not to notice how little hair she has left. Her lips are livid, almost cadaverous, and her neck is thin. And she has bulging veins and a nose that is long, much too long. However, there is one attractive feature about her: she is tall and bears herself very erect. And then her rump, they say, is soft and white, and the skin between her thighs is entirely hairless. It is as smooth as your face. And you will concede that she has a fascinating smile.

GLYKERA

So you believe that it is for her beauty that the Arcanian loves her? You don't know, then, that her mother is the sorceress Chrysarion. The witch knows the Thettalian charms and can make the moon come down to earth. People say she flies in the air by night. It was the sorceress who must have turned the soldier's head. She has made him drink certain magic potions. And now that Gorgona hugs him between her legs.

THAIS

And your voluptuous little legs, my Glykera, will hug another. But you may say goodbye to this man!

THE PHILOSOPHER

CHELODONION, a courtesan
DROSIS, her courtesan friend
NEBRIS, a slave

THE PHILOSOPHER

CHELIDONION

So little Clinias has stopped visiting your house? I haven't seen him for some time.

DROSIS

It is true, Chelidonion. His master has shut him up in their rooms. He stops the boy from coming to see me.

CHELIDONION

Whom are you talking about? You don't mean Diotimos who is teaching at the gymnasium? Diotimos is a good friend of mine.

DROSIS

No; I refer to the most debauched of philosophers, Aristainetos.

CHELIDONION

You mean the long-faced, funereal man with the shaggy whiskers? He takes the little fellows for walks thru the Poikile.

DROSIS

Yes, that is the faker. I wish he'd die in a hurry! May the executioner drag him to his peace by his whiskers!

CHELIDONION

But how could a character like this false philosopher have seduced Clinias?

DROSIS

I don't know, Chelidonion. The boy hasn't set his foot in my street for the last three days; I am rather worried. It was I, you know, who taught him what woman is; and he hasn't slept with another woman since his first lesson. Having bad presentiments in regard to my Clinias, I sent Nebris, my slave, to see if he was at the Agora or in the Poikile. Nebris tells me she saw him walking with Aristainetos. She nodded to the boy from a distance, and Clinias blushed and was discomfited but did not look at her again. Then they reëntered the city. Nebris followed as far as the Dipylon, but, since they did not come out again, she returned without learning anything more.

You can imagine how worried I have been since then. I don't know what will become of the boy. I have always treated him fairly. At first I was afraid some other woman had got him and his love for me had turned to hate. It also seemed possible that his father forbade him to see his Drosis. This evening, however, Dromon, the boy's slave, came to me with this letter. Take it and read, Chelidonion. You can read, can't you?

CHELIDONION

Let us see now. The penmanship is not especially good. You can see this letter was written in a hurry. He writes:

Oh, how much I love you, my Drosis! The gods, every one of them, will vouch for the degree of my affection. Know, therefore, that it is not by reason of dislike but by necessity that I have come to be separated from you. My father has intrusted me to Aristainetos to study philosophy, and my master has found out everything about the two of us and has scolded me severely, saying it was not meet for the son of Architeles and Erasicleia to carry on with a courtesan. He says that he will convince me that virtue is preferable to voluptuousness.

DROSIS

May the imbecile suffer an apoplectic fit! Think of teaching such philosophy to a young man!

CHELIDONION

So that I am forced to obey my master. He follows me wherever I go and guards me carefully and lets no woman approach me. He promises me that if I learn his kind of wisdom and do what he requires of me, I shall, after some efforts, become a virtuous and happy man. I write this letter hurriedly. I hope no one is looking.

Be happy and think sometimes of your,

Lost forever,

CLINIAS.

DROSIS

What do you think of the letter, Chelidonion?

CHELIDONION

The words of an uncultivated Scythian, Drosis. However, the last two lines suggest some possibilities. All in all, in my opinion, your Clinias will never become a great poet.

DROSIS

That's what I think, too. But I am dying for the little fellow's love. He is like a kitten. Dromon tells me that Aristainetos is reputed to have a weakness for young boys. That is, under the pretext of teaching them rhetoric and philosophy, the whiskered codger lives with the most handsome of his pupils. According to Dromon, Aristainetos has already had an interesting conversation with Clinias on the subject and promises to make the boy like to the gods. He reads to him of the love affairs that the old philosophers had with their disciples, and tells him that the gods don't interest themselves in women, but prefer the company of good philosophers like himself. However, Dromon threatens to complain to the boy's father.

CHELIDONION

Dromon is good. We ought to reward him, Drosis. DROSIS
I have already done it, though there is little need of a gift to win him to my side. My Nebris, you know, rather tickles the slave's fancy.

CHELIDONION

In that case, do not worry, Drosis. Everything will turn out fine. In my opinion you ought to leave an inscription on the part of the Keramic wall where Architeles takes his daily walk. He will understand the danger his son is in and will save him from his doom.

DROSIS

But shall we be able to write without being seen?

CHELIDONION

It will be done at night, Drosis, with a piece of charcoal that we shall pick up on the way.

DROSIS

Fine! Stand with me, Chelidonion, in my fight against the pedant. We courtesans must not allow those whiskered philosophers to mislead the young generation.

Milton Keynes UK
Ingram Content Group UK Ltd.
UKHW022015310723
426115UK00005B/320